A BRIDE FOR A DEBT

MAIL ORDER BRIDES OF TEXAS

SUSANNAH CALLOWAY

Tica House
Publishing

Sweet Romance that Delights and Enchants!

PERSONAL WORD FROM THE AUTHOR

Dearest Readers,

Thank you so much for choosing one of my books. I am proud to be a part of the team of writers at Tica House Publishing who work joyfully to bring you stories of hope, faith, courage, and love. Your kind words and loving readership are deeply appreciated.

I would like to personally invite you to sign up for updates and to become part of our **Exclusive Reader Club**—it's completely Free to join! We'd love to welcome you!

Much love,

Susannah Calloway

VISIT HERE to Join our Reader's Club and to Receive Tica House Updates:

https://wesrom.subscribemenow.com/

CONTENTS

CHAPTER 1

Staring at the letter in front of him, Donald Bailey rubbed his lips with a hand that trembled badly. Craving a drink, his eyes flashed to the whiskey bottle on the sideboard. Alma would see the level dropping, the golden liquid inside less than when she saw it last. Her eyes would narrow, she would hover near enough to smell it on his breath.

He hated her judgmental eyes. *Who is she to judge me? I married her when no one else would. I took her in when the father of her unborn daughter abandoned her. I gave Serena my name.* Despite his inner protestations, Donald realized, deep inside, she was right to hold him to account.

Looking back at the letter, phrases leapt out at him. *Repay the loan. Face the consequences. I will marry your stepdaughter.* Unable to resist the bottle's call, he rose from his chair and paced to the sideboard. His hand shook so badly, he splashed some of the whiskey onto the tray as he poured. He had no sooner taken a sip when Alma walked in.

"Imbibing early," she sniped, folding her hands in front of her skirts in the way that never failed to annoy him. "It's no wonder we're going bankrupt—your drinking, your gambling."

"Silence, woman."

"Why should I be silent?" Alma demanded. "It's my life you're ruining along with your own. Mine *and* Serena's."

I will marry your stepdaughter. Consider the loan paid in full.

Returning to his armchair, Donald ignored his wife's accusing gaze, thinking quickly as he sipped the whiskey. The liquor helped to calm some of the trembling in his hands, clarified his mind. If he sent Serena to Texas to be Hubert Bishop's bride, the money he owed the man would no longer be owed. The debt would be paid in full.

Manna from heaven.

"Donald, what is it?"

He glanced up to see Alma striding toward him, her judgmental expression altered to one of concern.

"Serena is twenty-one years old now," he said, his voice hoarse. "She should be married."

Alma folded her arms across her stomach, and Donald observed that his shaking had miraculously transferred itself to her. "And?"

"Hubert Bishop offered to cancel our debt to him if Serena married – his son." Donald cut his eyes away from Alma's at the blatant lie. Hubert had no son. *They will never know until it's too late.* "His son needs a wife, and Serena needs a husband."

"She can find a husband here."

Donald shook his head, emphatic. "She is beautiful, yes, but many women are going west to find marriageable husbands. New York is no place for her. Young Bishop will treat her well. She will have money and status in Texas."

God grant she not find out Hubert's true disposition until after the wedding. If he treats his wife the way he treats his horses, Serena will wish she'd never been born. Of course, he could not tell Alma that, nor Serena. His conscience twitched at the thought that he would sell Serena with no more thought than he'd sell a broodmare, but his craven need to be out from under the crippling debt tormented him.

Alma sat down in a chair, her face filled with doubt. "This doesn't seem right, Donald. Serena should have a choice in her husband."

"Think of being out from under Hubert's thumb," he insisted, feeling sweat spring from his brow. "We need not be bankrupt after all. And Serena will be cared for all the days of her life."

The lie tasted sour on his tongue, but he ignored it. "We must tell her the good news."

Striding to the door, Donald called, "Serena, will you come in here for a few minutes."

Alma sat, staring at her hands, neither protesting nor looking pleased with Donald's handling of the situation.

As long as she keeps her silence. He returned to his chair, his comfort within his lies growing. The truth didn't matter. All that mattered was his newly secured future, and Serena married.

He watched Serena enter the room over the rim of his whiskey glass. He trembled not at all as he lifted his hand to beckon her, thinking that with her gone, he'd no longer need to feed or clothe her, or buy her useless books.

"Come in, child," he told her expansively. "Your mother and I have good news to share."

Where she had gotten her nearly perfect beauty, Donald never knew. Alma certainly never had that petite, tiny frame with a waist so slim he could put his hands around it and his fingers would meet. Nor did she have those striking green eyes, nor that hair of fire roped into a thick braid that fell almost to her hips.

Serena looked to her mother first, and clearly observed that whatever the good news was, Alma didn't share it. "What is it, Donald?"

Though he had given her his name and raised her from an infant, Donald knew Serena had never taken to him, and never once called him, "Father."

"A dear friend of mine has requested your hand in marriage, my dear," Donald told her, enjoying his new freedom and his whiskey. "It is time for you to have a family of your own."

Donald glanced at Alma to find her staring at her hands. Serena's face paled slightly, and she licked her lips nervously. "Marriage? To someone here in New York?"

"Not quite. Hubert and his son live in Texas."

"Texas!"

"El Paso to be exact." Donald enjoyed Serena's distress. "You will marry his son. My old friend has great wealth and status, and you will want for nothing."

"How could you just hand me over to some – friend?" Serena demanded. "I have the right to choose my own husband."

"Not while you are my daughter," Donald snapped. "There is nothing for you here, child. The only marriageable husbands in New York are dock workers and foreign laborers. Hubert's son is kind, I am told, even handsome."

"Mother?"

Donald watched through narrowed eyes; his palms sweaty as Alma lifted her face toward her daughter. If Alma spoke of the cancelled debt, he knew Serena would instantly refuse. If that happened, he would be ruined. In his letter, Hubert demanded either the full amount paid, plus interest, or Serena's hand.

Donald had no way of paying the debt and could not possibly get a loan from a bank to cover it.

"He is right, Serena," Alma said wearily. "This is a prime opportunity for you to marry a wealthy gentleman of substance."

"A man whom I have never met. A stranger."

"Marriages have been arranged between strangers since the dawn of time," Donald told her, his tone unctuous. "In order to extend family ties."

Serena stared at him with contempt. "Do you hate me that much?"

His mouth agape, Donald spluttered. "Of course not. I'm thinking of your welfare, child."

"You haven't ever considered anyone's welfare outside of your own."

Turning, Serena stalked from the room, leaving Donald to blink at her erect back.

CHAPTER 2

Cantering his black and white horse across the dry, desert scrubland, Nartan glanced at the two gutted deer on the packhorse. The beasts were fat from grazing on the sage and thin grass and would be welcomed by his grandmother. At his side galloped his friend, Bodaway, whose quick bow had brought down not just a deer, but also two plump rabbits.

"Your father has spoken of turning leadership of the tribe over to you," Bodaway commented.

Nartan eyed him sharply. "What is this?"

"You have not heard? He spoke of it to my father."

"No, I have not." Nartan gazed out over the sandy plains dotted with prickly pear, sage, and the occasional thicket of short stubby trees. "Perhaps I have not given him the opportunity, either."

"Ah." Bodaway's cheerful grin bloomed wide. "You would make a great chief, my friend."

"I have no wish to be one," Nartan replied. "Being chief means responsibility I do not want."

"There is no other the people will accept," Bodaway told him, his grin fading. "You are respected as a hunter and as a warrior. Just as your father is."

Nartan chewed his lower lip. "My father is not yet aged," he said slowly. "But old wounds pain him greatly, especially in the winter rains. I had hoped he would bear his burden for years, and not place it upon me."

Ahead of them, smoke from the cooking fires rose in the distance, and the tips of the village wickiups poked over the desert scrub. As they rode closer, they were seen, and a small number of children ran to greet them. Though she was hardly a child, Cocheta strolled forward to meet them halfway, her smiling eyes on Bodaway.

She was eighteen, and she had already chosen him. After courting the last few months, Bodaway was almost ready to make offers to her family. Deeply in love, they scarcely spent time apart from one another. Leaving them to talk, Nartan reined in near his grandmother's tent, and slid down from his pony.

Gouyen emerged from behind the flap, a diminutive woman with a face as wrinkled as a winter dried apple, yet her dark eyes gleamed with knowledge and youth. She watched Nartan untie the deer from the packhorse, and stepped forward, closer to the fire.

"Ayee, we will feast this night," she declared in her raspy voice. "You have done well, hunter."

Nartan grinned as he wrangled one of the deer to lay at her feet. "The hides will keep you warm this winter, Grandmother."

"I have furs in plenty, Nartan," she answered. "But I am in need of leather for clothing."

"Then here you have more than enough."

Gouyen peered up at him. "Your father wishes to see you, Grandson. You cannot avoid him forever."

Nartan set the other deer down, avoiding her glance. "He wishes me to be chief," he said softly.

"Is that such a bad thing?"

"I am not ready."

Her wrinkles doubled as Gouyen smiled. "By those words I believe you are. Go. He is down by the river. Your sister will be here shortly to help me skin and cut these up."

Vaulting onto his horse's bare back, Nartan reined him

around and nudged him into a gallop amid the wickiups and out of the village. Dread rode with him, and he wished he was rebellious enough to ignore his father's summons. But he could not disrespect his father and the chief of the people.

Mangas stood on the bank of the river, fishing with a thinly braided line as Nartan rode up and dismounted. He did not glance up as Nartan paced forward to stand beside him. "You were successful in your hunt?" Mangas asked.

"Two deer, Father."

"Your prowess as a hunter brings you much respect."

Nartan eyed the three gleaming trout lying in the grass beside the deeply flowing river. "It would appear your prowess as a fisherman exceeds mine as a hunter."

"Bah." Mangas snorted. "I desired fish for my dinner. And your grandmother craved some, so I would honor her wishes."

As Nartan watched, Mangas jerked his line, the thin cord taut, and a silvery fish leaped from the water, struggling against the hook in its mouth. Mangas carefully pulled the trout in, and held it up, flapping wetly, for his son's inspection. He grinned.

"That should be enough for our dinner," he said with satisfaction.

"You wished to see me?"

Grasping the still struggling fish, Mangas removed the hook from its gasping mouth. "You seemed eager to avoid me."

Nartan gazed across the river. "Not you, but your words I have no desire to hear."

"Ah. I would have you hear my words. You must marry."

Nartan squatted on the bank and threw small pebbles into the water. "None of the maidens have caught my eyes."

"You have caught theirs." Mangas chuckled and lay the trout down with the others. "They watch you with hope, my son. They quarrel with one another for the right to stand forth in the effort to make you pick one of them as your wife. Any one of them will bring you honor."

Throwing a rock forcefully into the river, Nartan spoke with heat. "I have honor. I want love."

"This does not mean you will not love your wife," Mangas informed him, squatting beside him. "I did not love your mother when we married, but it was not long before I did. She was a good wife, obedient, and gave me two beautiful children."

"I will marry in time," Nartan said, glancing sidelong at Mangas. "I do not wish to right now. Nor do I want to take your place as chief."

"My bones pain me," Mangas said, his voice low. "I am stiff

where once I was limber. The people have the right to have a leader who is strong."

"You *are* strong."

"Once I was. Past injuries have caught up to me, and now I cannot ride a horse without great pain. I do not ask you to replace me right now, Nartan. But soon. The people will accept you as chief. You have counted coup on our enemies. You are brave, a true warrior. It is my wish that you decide on a bride."

CHAPTER 3

Serena came quite close to running away. Had she the funds to escape Donald's terrifying decision to marry her to his friend's son, she would have packed her things and gone to pay a permanent call on her cousin in Pennsylvania. Yet, she did not have the money.

Rebellious, scared, she had hardly spoken to either Donald or her mother in the weeks since she'd been informed she would marry in El Paso, Texas. "I daresay the place can hardly call itself civilized," she snapped under her breath as she packed her belongings.

Serena had no qualms about blaming her mother for this atrocity. "Donald knows what is best for you," Alma had told her time and again, but Serena didn't believe it then, nor did she believe it now.

"Why didn't you stand up to him, Mother?" Serena had nearly hollered in her mother's face. "How could you agree to this?"

Guilt whipped her sharply at the agony she saw on her mother's face. Alma had never appeared old to her – not until that moment. Alma stared down at her hands.

"You must marry someone," her mother whispered. "A young man of wealth and prestige is a godsend."

"Maybe to you," Serena snapped, striding away. "Right now, I'd be far happier with marrying a dock worker who doesn't speak English. At least it would be my choice."

Now she packed her satchels, took her favorite books, a little jewelry, and almost ignored a small portrait of her mother in her younger years. She tucked it in, then added her Bible, and mementos she knew she would miss if she left them behind.

A small rap at her door announced her mother. Serena didn't turn as Alma came in. "Donald hired a coach to take us to the train station," Alma said, her voice quiet, hushed.

"Just where did he find the money for it?" Serena asked, cold.

Alma came around to stand in front of her. "You are still angry with me."

"Yes, I am." Serena did not look up.

"How much choice do you think I have, Serena?'

Serena glanced at her mother, at the desperation, the fear, in her voice. "What do you mean?"

"Do you think I *want* to send my only child across the country and perhaps never see her again? At least, you will be free of him. I must remain and be a dutiful wife to a man I despise."

Guilt at the cold-hearted treatment she had given her mother in the past weeks tore at her heart. Tears filled her eyes. "I am so sorry, Mother. Forgive me."

Alma smiled though her tense, bitter expression. "I must beg your forgiveness, Serena, for ever marrying that monster. I had little choice. I could not raise you alone and he was the only one who offered marriage."

Sitting on the edge of the bed, Alma gazed out the window. "I was soiled. I was bearing another man's child while not married to him. I took the first offer that came along."

"I know." Serena sat beside her and took her hand. "My father should have stayed and taken care of you, given you and me a future."

Alma laughed. "Oh, he couldn't have done that. The thought of a commitment to a wife and baby made him break out in hives."

Squeezing her hand, Alma smiled into her eyes. "For all of Donald's faults, and yes there are so many of them, we should be grateful he never beat us."

Her mother's words sent a shiver through Serena, as though a chill wind blew through her soul. "Yes," she replied slowly, "we must be grateful for the roof over our heads he provided, the food we ate."

"And I was not on my hands and knees scrubbing floors for a few coins a week," Alma added, then put her arm around Serena's shoulders. "Will you write to me? Tell me how you are?"

Serena kissed her cheek. "Of course, I will."

"Perhaps your husband will not be a drinker nor a gambler," Alma said. "You may find a perfectly handsome, kind and loving man waiting for you in the West."

Serena tried not to roll her eyes as she rose to continue packing. "What sort of people live in a place called El Paso, Texas? Nothing but cowboys, Mexicans, and Indians from what I've heard."

"If I did not have hope for you, Serena," her mother told her sadly, "I would never permit this."

"I know," Serena replied. "I will try to find some hope as you do."

Serena said nothing on the carriage ride across the big city of New York. She merely gazed out the window at the passing people and traffic. She wondered if El Paso was as sprawling and ugly as New York, and if it was filled with people from across the world who spoke dozens of different languages.

At least, Donald kept his mouth shut during the ride, hopefully from shame. Had he spoken to her, she had no idea what she might have said to his face. Alma held her hand the entire trip, often patting it, as though wanting to never let Serena leave her side.

At the station, Donald carried her bags and hamper that held enough food to last her all the way to Texas. Serena stared at him, her face devoid of expression, as he paused in front of her. She wondered if he expected an embrace, a word of love or comfort, from her. *If he does, he'll be terribly disappointed.*

In the end, Donald walked back to the carriage, his head low. Alma took Serena into her arms, and Serena saw she was crying. "Be strong, my Serena," she whispered, swallowing her tears. "I love you so much."

Tears rolled down Serena's cheeks before she thought to hold them back. "I love you, Mother. Pray for me, please."

"Every day. I will miss you, and ache for you, my sweet child."

That broke Serena down. She sobbed in her mother's arms, weeping as though she were small again and had scraped her knee.

"Come back," Alma told her through her own sobs. "If things are bad for you, come home. You can always come home."

"I will do that." Serena pulled away and fumbled for a

handkerchief to wipe her face with. "And I will write you, Mother, as often as I can."

"And I will watch for the postman every day."

Serena hugged her again, whispering, "Take care of yourself."

"Of course."

A porter came by, asking if that was her luggage, tipping his small hat.

"Yes, it is."

"Which train, miss?"

"Uh, the one for El Paso. That's in Texas."

"Yes, miss. It's that train right there. You'll have to change trains later, but that's the one to be on. It leaves in ten minutes."

He pointed to a train, then took her bags with him, leaving the hamper of food. Alma watched him go, then took Serena into her arms again. "You better go. If you stay any longer, I won't have the courage to say goodbye."

"Nor will I have it to leave." Serena kissed her mother's cheek. "Goodbye, Mother."

"Goodbye, Serena. You are strong, but I will send my strength to you."

Picking up the heavy hamper, Serena walked toward the

train, feeling as though her heart would break—and that she would never see her mother again this side of heaven.

~

Serena was unprepared for the sheer agony of the cross-country journey. The train car stifled her despite some open windows. It rocked ceaselessly, rendering sleep nearly impossible for the first few nights. Glad she had kept some books out of her satchels, she was able to read and not grow too terribly bored with so little to do.

Her fellow passengers were mostly men, who eyed her sidelong as though they had never seen a woman before. What few women who were on the train, with their husbands, took her under their wings and helped her to feel more comfortable.

"You will love the West," one stout matron named Maud told her. "It is so clean. You can breathe the fresh air, and you do not have to endure the dreadful stench of New York."

Serena laughed. "I expect you have been to New York?"

"I grew up there, dear. Never want to go back." Maud leaned toward her as though imparting a confidence. "Jack and I are going to Denver, in Colorado Territory. He is taking a position with the territorial government. There's talk of making it a state in a few years."

"And I am bound for Texas."

"Well, dear," Maud told her. "I have never been to Texas, but I am told it has nothing but long horned cattle and cowboys. Are you to marry a cowboy?"

Serena shook her head. "I have never met him."

"You are so pretty," Maud said, patting her hand. "I am sure he will love you."

I am not so sure about that.

Maud and her Jack got off the train in St. Louis to board another bound for Denver, Maud waving to her through the windows. Serena silently blessed the woman for her kindness. She herself would get off the train in Oklahoma City, where this one would continue straight west, while hers would meander through Oklahoma and Texas before finally arriving in El Paso.

As often as possible, Serena would disembark the train to walk around at the various stops, craving the exercise and stretching her legs. Trying not to stare, she would see Indians and Mexicans and listen to the different languages spoken around her. The Indians, especially, fascinated her, for she had read about the savages in the papers and dime books.

Yet, if they were savage, they displayed none of it. They walked like everyone else, even though they wore leather garb decorated with feathers and small beads. A few had weapons, and some were women in long dresses, not unlike her own. Their black hair appeared almost blue in the sunlight, and their dark coppery skin held Serena entranced. *This isn't much different than New York, where immigrants come from all parts of the world, bringing with them their dress, cultures, and languages.*

Serena's body adjusted to sleeping on the rocking train, and she spent many hours gazing at the passing scenery. In Texas, she saw the mighty long-horned cattle she had read about. The vast spread of their horns from point to point made her gasp in awe. Traveling from the rich and green lands of Oklahoma and northern Texas, the landscape changed to drab browns and grays. Only stubby trees grew. She recognized the desert-type landscape, and it became frightfully hot.

"This is where I'm spending the rest of my life?" she asked herself, dismayed by the long miles of emptiness.

At last, the train's whistle blew, and the chugging wheels slowed to a crawl. From the train, the city of El Paso appeared to be just like any other frontier town she had passed through since leaving New York, and she valiantly tried to stifle her disappointment.

"Nothing but cattle and cowboys," she muttered, rising from her seat.

The air felt as though she had walked into an oven and sweat poured down from her brow under her bonnet. Even so, Maud was right. It didn't have the horrid stench of New

York, nor the pressing crowds, nor the thick traffic of horses and wagons. A breeze blew up, and cooled her, smelling of sage and desert.

"Are you by chance Miss Serena Bailey?"

Turning, Serena found herself looking at a handsome young man about her own age. He had bright blue eyes, tawny hair and a smile that brought one to her own lips. *Perhaps marriage won't be so horrible after all.* "Yes, I am. Are you Hubert Bishop's son?"

He tipped his cowboy hat, still smiling. "Oh, no, Ma'am. I'm Charles. I work for Mr. Bishop, and he sent me to collect you."

"Oh. I see."

Disappointment filled her, but Serena blinked away the tears and fought against the nervousness as Charles struggled under the weight of all her luggage. "This way," he said. "I have a wagon."

Following him to a long wagon drawn by a pair of the ugliest mules Serena had ever seen, she waited, wondering how she was supposed to get up into that high seat. Charles placed her belongings in the back, then helped her up, her hand in his.

"Mr. Bishop's place is about a mile outside of town," he told her, slapping the mules' rumps with the reins. "He runs cattle, and manages the bank, though he don't own it."

"What is his son like?"

Charles eyed her sidelong. "Ma'am?"

"His son," Serena persisted. "The one I am supposed to marry."

He swallowed visibly. "Why, Ma'am, he ain't got no son."

CHAPTER 4

"I am not ready to marry."

Nartan walked through the village with Bodaway, watching the giggling young women who stared at him boldly, waving to get his attention.

"Why not? Look at them," Bodaway said with a gesture. "All of them are beautiful, and they will bear you strong sons. All of them can cook, dress out a deer, tan hides, sew your breeches. Not a one of them has a reputation for laziness. You should pick one."

Eyeing them from the corner of his eye, Nartan knew, that while what his friend said was correct, none of them attracted him at all. "Perhaps next year," was all he said.

"And by next year, the other warriors will have married them," Bodaway protested. "There will be none left for you."

"Then if that happens, it happens."

Bodaway remained silent for a while. "You go to the council meeting now?" he asked.

"Yes. My father wants me to attend from now on. He wants to begin teaching me about how to lead the village."

"Then I must part from you." Bodaway clasped Nartan's forearm in brotherly friendship. "I will see you soon."

As the weather was fair, the council meeting would not be held in a wickiup, but near the river. He slowly approached the group of five men, including his father, as they sat cross-legged on the ground. He waited, polite, for an invitation before his father beckoned him with a wave of his arm.

"Sit here beside me," Mangas told him. "We were just speaking of you."

Nartan nodded greeting to the old men, considered wise among the people. They wore, as he and his father did, shirts of light cotton due to the heat, leather breeches with loin cloths, and long strips around their heads to hold back their hair. Beads, for luck, had been sewn into their clothing, and all wore long knives at their belts.

Nartan felt their eyes on him, weighing, judging, before one turned to his father and said, "He has not the maturity we need in our chief, Mangas. He is yet frivolous and should settle down with a wife before becoming chief."

Mangas nodded gravely. "I agree, Kuruk. I will remain chief while I teach my son wisdom and convince him to marry."

"I am not ready for either," Nartan told them. "I have no wish for my father to step aside."

"You have some wisdom, Nartan," Eknath admitted. "I like how you freely speak of your lack, but under your father's tutelage, you will grow."

Nartan bowed his head. "I will learn all my father and you have to teach."

The council then spoke of the nearby town of El Paso, the ranchers and their cattle encroaching on Apache lands. "We should move the village," Eknath proposed. "Head north and away from the whites."

Mangas shook his head. "I dislike moving so far from water. It is the dry season, there has been no rain for many weeks. The whites have not troubled us, and we have peace with the town. I say we have patience and wait until closer to winter before going north to the buffalo."

Kuruk agreed. "The whites are not our friends, nor are they our enemies. When the rains come, then we will move. Remember the traders who came from there, parched for lack of water?"

"We are at peace, but how long will that last?" Eknath continued. "We can make camp by the small creeks that run out of the mountains."

Nartan watched his father glance at the other councilors. "What do you say?"

"We have water, and good hunting," replied Itza-Chu. "Our women have foraged for nuts, fruits, corn and beans. Unless the white men from town create problems, I believe we should stay."

The other two also voted to remain, and Nartan carefully watched Eknath's face for any hint of his thoughts. If he hated the prospect of staying, none of it showed on his peaceful expression.

"Then we remain here until the rains come," Mangas declared. "As long as the hunting remains good, we will resist the temptation to raid the cattle."

"Perhaps we might trade for a few head of cattle," Itza-Chu commented. "That rancher to the west, Henderson, he is open to talk trade with us."

Mangas frowned. "What do we have that he may want?"

"My wife tanned some beautiful elk hides," Itza-Chu answered with a grin. "Henderson likes them in his wood house."

Mangas looked at Nartan. "Then perhaps going to talk to

Henderson might be a good experience for you. I think there may be many women who have hides to trade for beef."

~

With Bodaway and a few other young warriors, Nartan led a pack horse with several hides tied to it, riding west into white man territory. He had met this Henderson a few times, and found him strange, but pleasant enough. As they rode, they kept a watchful eye out for the cowboys that guarded the herds, and who might misconstrue their peaceful intentions.

The cowboys of Henderson's tribe waved to them as they passed, and Nartan's small band waved back. "I am glad we are at peace," Bodaway commented with his usual grin. "War makes it difficult to marry and make babies."

Nartan laughed. "Is that all you think about anymore?"

"If you were in love, that is all you would think about, too."

Henderson was in his wood structure amid the many barns and corrals that housed horses, cattle, pigs, goats. Nartan's horse nearly stepped on chickens that didn't get out of the way in time. The rancher emerged to stand on his shaded porch. He offered the Apache sign of peace. Nartan returned it.

"What can I do for you boys," he called, stepping down toward them. "Nartan, isn't it?"

"Yes, Henderson," Nartan replied in English. He slid down from his pinto and led the packhorse forward. Clasping the white man's arm in friendship, he gestured toward the hides. "We have splendid hides to offer you, if you are interested in trading."

"You do, eh?"

Henderson, a tall, aged man with a thick mustache that drooped past his chin, and bright blue eyes, wandered to the pack horse. He lifted the hides, examining them, offering polite nods to the warriors still mounted. "Yes," he said slowly, "these are nice. Quality workmanship."

Turning to Nartan, he said, "Cattle?"

"Yes, Henderson."

Henderson lowered his head to ponder. "I will take the hides in trade for four yearling heifers."

Nartan replied. "Seven."

Henderson gaped. "The hides are good, but they aren't that good. "Five heifers."

"Yearling heifers cannot feed that many of my people," Nartan replied. "Six and you throw in ten chickens."

Henderson laughed. "You know me too well, boy. Six heifers and ten chickens, it is. Come up on the porch, all of you. We'll drink to our trade."

One of the reasons Nartan liked Henderson was that he offered them cool tea to drink and sat on the wood floor of the porch with them, not on a chair. Bodaway took the hides from the horse and set them on the chairs before sitting cross-legged on the planks of the porch.

Henderson's wife served them the tea, smiling happily and asking after their health, and that of the village. Nartan drank the sweet tea, half wondering if they should trade for the tea and the secret to making it. As they drank, Henderson spoke of El Paso and the trouble the Mexicans were causing once they crossed the border.

"They still think Texas belongs to them," Henderson snapped. "We sent Santa Ana packing, and Texas is ours, not theirs. They cross the border, raiding our cattle and running them back south. They haven't hit my herds, but I know of several ranchers who *have* been hit."

"Cross the border and steal them back," Nartan told him. "Take some of theirs as well."

Henderson laughed. "That will start a new war with Mexico, son. But I like it."

As usual at these meetings, Henderson spoke of happenings in the area, what the Army was up to, and the outlaws. "You boys be careful," he warned them. "There are outlaws operating in the El Paso region, looking to kill you. They have no love for your people."

Nartan nodded. "I am grateful for your information, Henderson. We will be careful."

"Keep your women close. They'd like nothing better than to hurt them, if you know what I mean."

His eyes went to his wife, who poured more tea into their glasses. Nartan observed the loving and protective look in the man's eyes and felt glad he wasn't married. He didn't want the added worry of a wife's safety.

"When the rains come," he said, "we will move to our northern hunting grounds."

"Before that happens," Henderson said with a grin, "come see me. Maybe we can work out another trade."

Nartan returned his grin. "We will, I am certain."

Thus, the chickens were shoved into burlap sacks, and the six yearling heifers herded back the long miles to the village.

"Did I make a good trade?" Nartan asked Bodaway.

"In my opinion," Bodaway replied with a grin, "yes. Six heifers will go a very long way toward feeding our people, and the chickens, well, they taste very good when turned into a soup."

Mangas was also quite pleased with the trade Nartan negotiated and suggested that they trade fresh venison for beef before they turned north for their winter camp. Two of the heifers were slaughtered while the others were turned loose to graze with the horse herd, under the watchful eyes of the warriors guarding them.

As Nartan sat before the fire that night, dining on fresh beef hot from the flames, he told his father about Henderson's warnings. "He said outlaws were in the area. We must guard our horses well."

Mangas nodded. "I, too, have heard of the lawless ones arriving from the north and the east. They will try to kill us if they can. As you hunt, my son, keep a watchful eye out. They would like nothing more than to start a war between us and the white men."

"Some of them are former soldiers from the white's army."

"Yes, from their states' war. Some only want money or food, but others hate us as much as they hate the black man and the Mexicans. Those men will try to kill us."

CHAPTER 5

Serena took a good look at the sprawling ranch house, the yard with chickens pecking and scratching the ground. She suppressed a shudder. The place was clearly not cared for, the horses in the corral were underweight, and paint peeled from the walls of both the barn and the house. Charles reined the mules in, then jumped to the ground.

The screen door to the house banged open just as Charles assisted Serena down from the seat. Her mouth dry as though she had swallowed sand, she looked at the man who strode across the shaded porch to lean against a post, returning her measured glance. Smoking a thin cigar, he lifted his hand to his mouth and pulled it from his lips.

The man watching her was clearly older than even Donald, with a face and expression, as hard as a granite block. His thin grey hair under a bowler hat waved gently in the light breeze, his dirt colored eyes stared at her with frank appraisal as well as a shine she didn't like at all. To say she felt dismayed was an understatement.

"You Serena?" he asked, his voice gritty.

"I am."

Behind her, she heard Charles removing her luggage from the back of the wagon, but she didn't take her eyes from the man on the porch. She had no doubt the man standing before her was dangerous.

"Come inside."

Turning, he strode back through the screen door, leaving her to wonder what would happen if she obeyed him. Would he hurt her? Fear and dread etched their way through her nerves. *I have no choice. I have no money, no place to go.* Forcing her feet to move, Serena strode slowly up the steps, Charles behind her with her satchels.

Hubert Bishop sat in a chair in the kitchen, smoking, watching as she entered and looked around. The smell of the unwashed dishes, crusted with old food and buzzing with flies, made her swallow hard. The floor needed a good sweeping, and the top of the stove was black with something Serena didn't want to know about.

Charles set the bags inside the door, then left without a word.

"I need a wife," Hubert stated without preamble. "We will marry tomorrow in front of the judge. You are virgin, I expect?"

Shocked at such a question, Serena had nothing to say. As though not really expecting an answer to that, Hubert continued, the shine in his eyes not abating a whit. "You'll provide me with a son, no useless daughters. You'll be expected to clean and cook, wash my clothes and keep house. You give me any trouble, and I'll beat you with a buggy whip."

Serena's eyes narrowed. "You hit me, and I'll go to the law."

Hubert snorted. "The law has nothing to say on the matter. You're my wife, bought and paid for."

"What do you mean?"

"Didn't ole Donald tell you?" Hubert chuckled, and it was not a nice sound. "I canceled his debt to me if he sent you here to be my wife. And he owed me a great deal of money."

Clenching her teeth, Serena gritted. "You can't marry me against my will. I will not marry you."

"What choice do you have, girl? Run back to town and become a tavern wench? Oh, yeah, you'll marry me, all right."

Hubert pointed behind him with his cigar. "Your room is back there. You'll start today by cleaning in here, and tomorrow morning we go to the judge to be married."

Not on your life.

~

Badly frightened, not knowing what else to do, and to give herself time to think, Serena put her bags in the bedroom Hubert had indicated. It had a very narrow bed with thin blankets, a bureau and nothing else in it save a lamp. The entire house was as dismal as the kitchen, and her bed gave off a rather musty, nasty odor.

Hubert didn't lift a finger to help her carry her bags, but rather watched her with that same calculating expression she didn't care for. Sitting on the edge of the bed, Serena stared into her very bleak future, wanting to swear, cursing Donald for doing this to her. *He flat lied about whom I was to marry. But he also knew that had he told the truth, I would have refused and never gotten on that train.*

Tears of self-pity rose to her eyes, despair filling her soul. *Why did this happen to me? Why would Donald send me into the hands of a man he knew was evil?* Stiffening her spine, Serena dashed the moisture from her face with the back of her hand. "There has to be an answer for me," she murmured. "Maybe if I go to the church in town and beg for sanctuary, the preacher will help me return to New York."

Feeling slightly better with that thought in mind, Serena stepped toward the kitchen and discovered Hubert was gone. Relieved by his absence, she stared at the mess, wrinkling her nose at the smell.

"He needs a maid more than a wife," she muttered.

Deciding that it wasn't worth her time to clean for him, Serena poked around the kitchen for something to eat. The afternoon waned toward early dusk, and she thought to sleep on the horrid bed for the night, then walk to town early in the morning. Finding nothing edible save some stale bread and dried beef, she munched on those, washing them down with water.

"What will I do with my things?"

Suddenly struck by the knowledge she couldn't carry all her bags to town with her, and unwilling to leave them with Hubert, Serena walked out of the house. Seeing no sign of Hubert, and nothing in the yard moving except the chickens, Serena walked around to the back.

Little, save dusty brown hills, pocked with thickets of scrubby trees, and big cactus-like plants met her inspection. Thinking to hide her satchels in a thicket not far away, she hoped Hubert would not think to look for either her or her possessions.

Making two trips, Serena did her best to hide her bags in the thicket of trees, adding dead branches to fully conceal them. "Now I can come back for them later, and he will, hopefully, presume I carried them to town with me."

Wishing she could do exactly that, Serena dusted her hands and clothes, then walked back to the house. The sun had sunk into the west, all but gone, but the light had not yet vanished as she entered the house, and stopped, frozen.

Hubert stared at her with a coldness, a terrible dark anger more terrifying than rage. His dirty eyes bore into her, and Serena's heart beat in heavy, thick strokes. "I told you to clean up this place," he said, his voice a low growl.

Serena lifted her chin. "You don't own me. And I'm leaving here."

Taking a sliding step toward her, Hubert lifted his hand. "You are going nowhere except to town with me. Now start my dinner, and after that, you will stay up all night cleaning this house."

"No."

The palm of his hand smacked Serena hard against her check, the force of the blow sending her reeling backward and into the stove. Stunned by his hitting her, as well as the pain, she stared at him in shock, her own hand touching her face.

"You hit me."

Hubert closed the distance between them, spittle slicking his lips. "I'll do it again if you give me any more of your sass."

Rage spread fiery fingers through Serena. "Only cowards strike women."

Hubert cracked his hand across her face again, snapping her head back. That only fueled her fury. Seizing a heavy cast-iron frying pan from the stove, Serena swung with all her strength. Caught by surprise, Hubert failed to duck in time. The pan cracked him on the side of his head, and he stumbled, crashing into the table.

He didn't fall. Knowing that if she lingered another minute, the man would kill her. Serena edged around him as Hubert held his head in his hands, blood squirting from between his fingers. *Run. Get out. Now.* Striding toward the door, Serena reached it just as Hubert seized a hold of her braid.

He yanked her back, but she still held the frying pan. Lifting it in time, she blocked another strike to her face, and Hubert bashed his knuckles on it. He let go of her braid and pulled a knife from his belt. Panic raced through her as he slashed the blade at her face.

Lifting the pan, Serena sought to once again block the knife coming at her. Partially successful, the blade cut her forearm, not her face or her throat. Hardly feeling any pain, she struck out again with the heavy pan, and succeeded in cracking him once again on the head.

This time, Hubert fell with a crashing thud to the floor. She whirled, knowing that if she were still there when he got up, she was dead. Running, Serena pushed the screen door and slammed her way through it, and across the porch. Thinking she'd get to the road that led into town, she bolted down the steps.

Two cowboys on horses stood there.

Too panic-stricken to see their stunned expressions, Serena turned and ran around the house. Thinking only of getting as far from Hubert as she possibly could, she ran into the desert, past the thicket where she had hidden her possessions, not stopping until she no longer had breath.

Pausing, she glanced back, half expecting to see Hubert and his men chasing her on horseback. In the half light of dusk, she saw nothing. No movement, no sounds of pursuit, only the moon rising in the east. Breathing hard with a terrible stitch in her side, Serena glanced down.

Blood covered her dress and was splashed over her bodice and down to her hem. Lifting her injured right arm, coated in red, the cut from Hubert's blade still oozed. It was deep, and the sight of all that gore sickened her. Bending, slightly dizzy, Serena tore long strips of cloth from her dress, and awkwardly bound her wound with her left hand.

Being right-handed didn't make the task any easier, and with the rush of fear leaving her, her injury began to hurt in earnest. Using her teeth as well as her fingers, she tied the cloth as best she could, hoping it was enough to stop her from bleeding to death.

Cradling her wounded arm in her healthy left hand, Serena gazed around into the near darkness. Predators came out at night, as did snakes, she realized. "Girl, you are in trouble deep," she muttered. She could not go back to Hubert's, for he would kill her. Walking out into the night might mean her death as well.

Caught between the two risks, Serena took the chance that she could travel the desert at night and survive. She would not survive another encounter with Hubert. In the distance, some creature yipped, and was joined by several others, and she shivered. "I don't know what you are, but I hope you're more scared of me, than I am of you."

Turning her back on the rising moon, Serena headed west, away from Hubert's ranch. As the moon waxed fuller and her eyes adjusted, she saw well enough to not walk into those ugly cactus piles. Though she didn't see anything that might slither, she did see several rabbits bolt from her presence.

Ignoring her pain as best she could, Serena walked on through the night. Many creatures ran from her, and she suspected she would be all right as long as they ran *from* her. If they ran *toward* her, she would most likely be killed. She felt cold, but walking kept her warm enough.

Thirst raged as she struggled on, and she didn't find any helpful creeks or ponds to assuage it. Facing the possibility she would not survive until morning, Serena prayed as she walked. She prayed for her mother, prayed for her own everlasting soul, prayed that when she died, it would be over quickly.

She walked for hours, growing exhausted as the moon chased her across the landscape. Her shoes were not made for walking, and her feet had grown painful blisters. Stumbling often, barely catching herself before she fell headlong to the ground, Serena gradually became aware of being followed.

Turning, she saw several dog-like animals a short distance away, sniffing the air, and she wondered if they were wolves. *I don't think those are wolves, but they are thinking of attacking me. I can see it.* The animals paused when she did, half circling her, watching.

Spotting a clump of trees a short distance from her, Serena edged toward it, keeping an eye on the beasts. Hoping that if she wiggled her way into the trees, she might be able to climb up some branches. Walking toward it, she picked up a stout piece of wood she could use if they attacked her.

The creatures kept their distance as she worked her way into the brambles and trees. Serena discovered that she could indeed climb up into the branches and perch there. Thorns scratched at her flesh and tore her dress, but she ignored the discomfort and settled on a heavier branch. She was only a few feet off the ground, but infinitely safer than being in the open where the beasts could come at her.

In the dark shadows among the branches, Serena couldn't

see them anymore. Parting the branches, she observed they were still there, sniffing the ground, staring at her. Yet, they seemed to know that going into the midst of the thicket to get at her might prove too dangerous for their safety. Who knew what other predators might be lurking about?

"That's right," she muttered. "You can't get me now. Go find some rabbits and leave me alone."

Not daring to sleep, Serena nonetheless rested, glad to not be walking, even if the tree was quite uncomfortable. *Come daylight, they'll go away, and I will continue on. Surely, I'll find a ranch hand or owner who will help me.* Leaning her head back on the tree's trunk, she gazed up at the sky and the stars.

Daylight is not far off. I'll be all right once dawn comes.

Serena dared not think of what might happen when the sun rose. The creatures would hopefully be gone, but she still had miles upon miles of open land to cross under the scorching sun. She had no water. *I won't make it past noon. But it is better to die out here than be murdered by Hubert Bishop.*

Birds chirped with the coming of the dawn, and the dog beasts didn't leave. Under the light of the new sun, Serena saw the grayish brown creatures with narrow muzzles and amber eyes that watched her with interest. Then it hit her. "They're waiting for me to die."

She couldn't leave the protection of the trees and brambles, or they would attack her. If she stayed where she was, she would die of thirst under the heat. "So that's it," she murmured. "I am to die out here. Lord Jesus, receive my soul, and bring me to the waters of heaven."

Gazing above her into the blue sky, she saw the circling vultures high overhead. "You'll have to fight those things for me," she told them. Serena tried not to think of the animals feasting on her corpse. "What will it matter? I'll be dead."

A horse snorted nearby.

Serena froze, staring as the dog creatures bolted, running in a pack to vanish below the hill. Hooves paced through the sandy soil toward her, and she caught the black and white flash of the horse's hide. Unable to believe her luck that someone, a person, rode a horse toward her and frightened the beasts away, Serena peered through the branches.

And came face to face with an Indian.

CHAPTER 6

Nartan, drawn by curiosity toward the coyotes, had wondered if they had trapped something in the mesquite thicket. Nearly unbelieving, he stared into the most incredible green eyes he had ever seen. The woman, a white woman, had hair like the fiery skies at sunset, yet was also covered in blood. *That's what attracted the coyotes.*

He studied her for a moment, observing her tension, her readiness to either fight or flee, the blood on her face. She carried a heavy stick in her hand, her preparedness to face death spoke to him of her warrior spirit.

"I will not hurt you," he told her in English.

That he spoke her tongue clearly startled her. She did not reply but watched him with the fierceness of a cornered badger. Nartan slid down from his pony, letting him graze on the grass as he made the Apache sign of peaceful intentions. Her tense expression showed him that she had no idea what that meant.

"I will not hurt you," he repeated. "I have water, I know you are thirsty."

"Do you plan to lure me out so you can kill me?"

Her voice had an interesting accent he had not heard among the whites before. Nartan cocked his head but offered her a small smile. "I would not offer you water if I planned to kill you. What is your name?"

"Serena."

"I am Nartan of the Apache. My village is not far away. You are hurt, and the blood smell on you will draw the coyotes."

"Is that what those were? Coyotes?"

Puzzled, Nartan gestured. "You do not know what a coyote is?"

"No. I'm not from around here."

"The coyote is the trickster, the thief. Under most circumstances, he is not dangerous. But you are weak and injured, so he will seek to kill you."

Noting the clumsy wrap on her injured arm, Nartan beckoned her. "Come, Serena. I will take you to my village.

49

My grandmother will ease your hurts, and you can eat and have something more to drink."

At last, Serena struggled down from the branch, and, ignoring the mesquite thorns, wriggled out of the thicket. She was tiny, smaller than most Apache maidens, and gazed up at him with a mixture of trust and suspicion on her face. "Thank you for helping me."

"You have the spirit of a warrior, Serena," he said. "You do not fear me."

"I came to terms with my death," she answered. "I am not afraid of it."

Picking her up, his hands around that tiny waist, Nartan set her on his horse. "As we ride, perhaps you might tell me how you came to be far from your people and hiding from the trickster in the mesquite."

Untying his water skin from his belt, Nartan handed it up to her. Serena guzzled the liquid as one parched. She drained the skin flask empty.

"I'm sorry," she told him, wiping her lips before handing it back. "I drank it all."

"Do not be concerned. We are not far from the village."

Grabbing a hold of his horse's mane, Nartan vaulted aboard behind her. Nudging the horse into a walk, he said, "I saw the vultures circling above," he said, "then the coyotes. I was curious as to what they had found, so I rode over."

"I am lucky you did."

"Who are your people?"

"I'm from New York," she replied. "A very long way from here."

Guiding the horse among the prickly pear and mesquite, keeping an eye out for potential trouble, Nartan wondered where New York was. He had never heard of it. "Where is that?"

"It took me eight days by train to get here," she answered, and he heard the amusement in her voice. "Very far to the northeast. It is a very big city."

"I know nothing of these cities. Why did you come?"

"I was to marry a man," she informed, her voice now angry. "My stepfather lied to me, sent me to marry a very bad man. An evil man. Hubert Bishop."

Nartan tensed. "I have heard of Bishop. He does not like my people."

"He hit me, and I fought him. He cut me, then I ran away. I walked all night until those creatures, the coyotes, made me take shelter in the trees. I thought I was going to die, so I made my peace with God."

"I know this Bishop is very mean. I do not blame you for not wanting to marry him."

"I would rather die than be with him."

"You are very brave for a white woman."

She laughed. "I don't take well to being hit."

"I would not, either."

They rode in silence for a time, Nartan beginning to like her as well as admire her. She was so small in his arms, yet as tough as a mesquite root. She seemed to be fearless, a fighter. His people admired such, and from what he knew about white women, they were timid and cowardly. *But then, I have not met many white women. Perhaps they are all like Serena.*

The village appeared in the distance, and he saw people shading their eyes as they gazed in their direction. Word obviously spread that he was not alone, for a small crowd gathered to gape. "My people will wonder why I am bringing you to the village."

"Will they be angry with you?"

Nartan chuckled. "No. We are a fierce people and proud, but we are also kindly and warm. You will be made welcome."

The villagers stared as he rode among them, gawking at the bloodied woman riding before him on his horse. He felt Serena's body stiffen, and he managed to lean forward enough to see her face. It was neutral, yet also without fear.

She did not smile, nor did she cringe as he reined in at Gouyen's wickiup.

He slid down, and caught her around the waist as she, too, lifted her leg over the horse's neck to drop lightly to the ground. Mangas and Kuruk strode through the crowd, looking from the woman to Nartan and back. Gouyen emerged from her wickiup, swiftly taking in Serena's injuries with her knowing eyes.

"Who is this woman, my son?" Mangas asked in Apache.

"I found her in a mesquite thicket," he answered, also in Apache. "Her name is Serena, and she was fleeing Hubert Bishop. It is he who injured her."

"It is good that you brought her to us," Gouyen told him, taking Serena by the arm. "I will take care of her."

Serena cast one backward glance over her shoulder at Nartan before following Gouyen inside, and out of sight. Kuruk waved his hands impatiently at the watching crowd, and they dispersed, talking about Serena's red hair and her green eyes. At Mangas's gesture, Nartan followed his father, leading his horse by the reins.

"Tell me all."

So Nartan told him everything he knew about her, as well as her fighting spirit, her lack of fear. "I could not leave her to the coyotes, my father," Nartan said firmly. "I will not regret bringing her to the village."

53

"Nor should you. Bishop will seek her, if he does not believe her already dead. But he is hated by his own people as well as the Apache. He is of no account."

"We must be wary of him, however," Kuruk advised. "He is poison."

"I will not fear him, for in truth, he is a coward." Nartan paced on beside his father, thinking. "Serena fought him when he struck her. He knows he cut her. He may believe she died in the desert."

"And then what?" Mangas stopped walking to gaze at Nartan. "Return her to the village of El Paso? He will find her there."

"The sheriff will protect her," Nartan replied. "Perhaps the white church, as well. Her people are from New York."

"I have never heard of such a place."

"Very far to the northeast," Nartan answered. "Eight days on the train."

Mangas exchanged an incredulous glance with Kuruk. "That is very far from here, indeed."

"I like her, Father."

Slightly defiant, Nartan met his father's eyes, unintimidated by Mangas's tight regard. Mangas said nothing for several moments, and Nartan could not read what he was thinking.

His father's normally benign and open countenance was closed, and he revealed nothing.

"We shall see," was all Mangas said.

~

Much later, Serena emerged from the wickiup with Gouyen. Nartan had hovered near through the long hours, half listening to the murmurs from inside, and the occasional laughter. Clad in a traditional Apache skirt, soft doeskin boots to her knees, and a beaded blouse, Serena gazed at Nartan in half challenge, half entreaty.

Gouyen had cared for Serena's arm, for it was bound in clean cloths. Her fiery hair had been brushed and re-braided and hung to her waist. To Nartan, he had never seen anyone so beautiful. He rose from his spot by the cook fire, staring, unable to look away.

Serena blushed under his rude gaze, smiling. "Gouyen said my gown was too bloody and would attract predators."

"It would," Gouyen said in English, and tossed her former clothes in the fire. "Her wound was deep, Grandson. You did right to bring her to me."

"The poultice she put on it eased the pain immediately," Serena told him, still smiling into his eyes. "She said she is the medicine woman of your people. The healer."

"Do you have a voice, Grandson?" Gouyen snapped in Apache. "Have you lost your wits?"

Nartan came to himself with a start. "Yes, Grandmother," he replied, grinning shyly. "I have lost them to this beautiful creature."

As though she understood him, Serena flushed a brighter pink, and gazed down. Gouyen poked him in the ribs, bringing his stare down to her, and he felt his own face grow hot with embarrassment.

"She is a guest," Gouyen said. "You are rude to our guest. Bring her food, Nartan."

"Yes, right away."

He trotted to his own wickiup and seized his long killing knife. Back outside, he quickly butchered a chicken, then lifted it high in his hands as he chanted a prayer of thanks to the creator and the spirit of the chicken. After plucking it, then gutting it, he took it back to Gouyen and Serena.

Spearing it over the fire, Nartan squatted, watching as Gouyen offered her nuts and pieces of squash. "You are hungry, Serena?"

"Very." Her eyes met his over the fire, and she smiled. "I have not eaten much lately."

"You are too thin," Gouyen chided her, poking her firmly in the ribs. "Apache maidens are not so thin."

If she was offended by the touch, Serena didn't show it. Instead, she nodded. "In New York, it's fashionable to be thin, with a small waist. We would wear corsets to make our waists look smaller."

Gouyen snorted. "What an unhealthy custom. People must have fat on their bones, or they might not survive a famine."

"We don't have famines in New York."

At Nartan's and Gouyen's insistence, Serena told of going to markets to get food, to pay for it with money (a sort of strange trade, Nartan suspected), and bringing it home to cook. "It can be delivered to your home, if you wanted," Serena added. "The very wealthy would not shop, they would have it delivered, or send their servants to get food."

"What a strange people you come from," Gouyen told her. "Your father never hunted? He was not a protector?"

Serena laughed. "My father abandoned my mother before I was born. My mother married Donald, who became my stepfather. And no, they never hunted. My stepfather hardly protected me, he sent me to an evil man."

Gouyen shook her head. "Such a terrible tribe, these people in New York." Leaning over, she patted Serena's knee. "Now you are among the right people, Serena. You must claim a man, let him know you are interested in him. If he wishes to marry you, he will buy you from your people."

Serena's expression, her eyes, grew a little wild. "I, er, had hoped to return to my people. In New York."

"They are too far away," Gouyen assured her. "We have many warriors in need of wives among the Apache. You claim one. Nartan will be chief, but he is lazy, and not a good provider."

Nartan felt his jaw drop. "Grandmother," he hissed. "I am a good provider, and a good choice for a husband. Why would you not say that?"

In Apache, Gouyen replied, "This girl must not pick from the one who saved her life. She must be shown other prospects. She must be permitted to choose. If she chooses you, you may buy her from her people."

"But her people are so far away."

Gouyen shrugged. "Then perhaps a family will adopt her. You may buy her from them."

Serena observed them conversing in in their tongue, trying to understand what they said. "You are looking for a wife, Nartan?" she asked.

"My father wishes me to marry," he replied. "I have not yet found a maiden I prefer."

"I see."

"And you rejected Bishop as a husband," he went on. "That is your prerogative, of course."

She gazed at him, curiosity in her strange green eyes. "Your women are permitted to choose their husbands?"

"Yes. If a warrior wishes to marry her, but she does not want him, she may reject him. Then he marries another. Is this not also the custom of your people?"

Serena stared at the fire. "Not always. My stepfather chose Bishop for me."

CHAPTER 7

Hubert limped into the telegraph office, his head aching from where Serena cracked him with the frying pan the night before. Dull fury still wracked him. He knew she was alive, even if she fled into the desert. He *knew* she had survived, and he would find her. And kill her.

"Help you?" asked the clerk.

Hubert dictated the message to acquaintances in New York, then paid for the message. He headed next to the bank where he worked, pleaded illness, and asked for money to be wired to New York. Only then was he free to go to the Gold Dust Saloon where he knew the tracker liked to drink.

Jake Simmons sat at a table playing cards with some dusty cowboys, their clothes still smelling like cattle dung. He glanced up briefly as Hubert's shadow fell over him yet continued playing through his hand until it was done, then scooted his chair back.

"What do you want?" he asked Hubert bluntly.

"Let's talk," Hubert said. "Over here."

Simmons picked up his winnings, then followed Hubert to a table in the corner. Hubert ordered whiskey from the saloon's wench and studied Simmons. The man was reputed to be the best tracker in Texas, yet he looked like a half breed Indian. He wore a headband like the Apache with stringy black hair and wore a white man's jacket. A six-gun hung low on his hip, his fingers never far from it.

"I need you to track someone," Hubert said. "Today."

"I'm busy."

"The wind might obliterate her tracks." Hubert winced over his next words. "I'll pay handsomely."

Simmons eyes narrowed. "How much?"

"Fifty dollars."

"You want urgency? That'll cost you a hundred. Up front."

Hubert cursed under his breath, but knew that if he wanted Serena found, alive, he needed Simmons to find her right away. Before the coyotes, or a snake, killed her. Scowling, he pulled out cash from his pocket and counted out a hundred dollars.

"Go to my place and pick up her tracks." Hubert glared at the tracker. "Bring her back to me."

With a sneering grin, Simmons tucked the cash away. "You're the boss."

Hubert drove his wagon, drawn by the mules, back to his ranch while Simmons rode his tall bay horse. "Who is she?" Simmons asked.

"My bride."

Simmons laughed. "She the one who belted you, gave you that knot on your head?"

"None of your business."

In his house, Hubert paced restlessly, drinking whiskey while Simmons followed Serena's tracks from the previous night. Hopefully, the wind had not eradicated them, and the tracker would bring her back. Or hopefully, drag her dead body behind his mount.

The day waned toward night by the time Simmons returned. Half drunk, Hubert met him on the porch as Simmons drew rein. He did not dismount.

"Did you find her?" Hubert demanded, squinting at the man.

Simmons gazed at him, expressionless. "No. Someone else did."

"What?"

"I tracked her across the desert," Simmons replied. "A man on a barefoot pony put her on his horse. She's with the Apache, Hubert."

Hubert felt his blood run cold. "No. That's impossible. *Impossible.*"

"Does she have red hair?"

Gazing up at him, Hubert nodded, mute. Simmons sighed, and took his hat off to scratch his head.

"I saw a young white woman with a red braid, dressed like an Apache, in their camp. I left, riding hard. Them Injuns might be peaceful at the moment, but I ain't gonna stick around if they decide not to be."

How in the blazes did she get mixed up with the Apache? Unable to think through the haze in his brain, Hubert struggled to speak. "You have to get her out. Go get her, Simmons."

The tracker laughed. "Tarnation, no, I ain't. I'm not gonna ride over there and demand your woman back. No, sir. You want her. You go get her yourself."

Putting his hat back on, Simmons reined his bay around and galloped out of Hubert's yard.

⁓

Never have I met so many cowardly men in my life.

For a week, Hubert talked to cowboys and drifters, outlaws and businessmen. Though he worked at the bank, his mind drifted to Serena, and his lust for vengeance increased. He would kill her with his bare hands, slowly strangle the life from her as her breath choked off, and her face turned red.

Yet, he could not fetch her back from the Apache without help.

And no one would agree, for any amount of money, to help him.

"I ain't stupid," said a dirty outlaw with a scraggly beard and no teeth. "Them Apache will kill me as soon as they look at me. Nawp. You get your woman back your own self."

Hubert knew he hadn't the skills of stealth or at arms to infiltrate the Apache village and bring Serena out without getting caught. And he knew exactly what the Apache did to whites who tried stealing their women. *Their women?* Was Serena an Apache now? Was she their captive, or one of them?

Hubert had no idea. The Apache kept to themselves, didn't bother El Paso or the ranchers, and seldom came into town. For all he knew, she was a slave to a warrior, and too useful in curing hides for her owner to want to surrender her to her lawful husband. Frustrated, angry, he drank too much, and went to the bank in the morning with raging hangovers.

The bank's owner watched him, and Hubert knew he watched.

After a week and a half, the train came into town with his New York associates on board, and with them was his leverage in getting Serena back.

Hubert smiled.

CHAPTER 8

If Donald drank to excess before Serena left, he now tripled his intake. Barely able to function, he did not go to his job as a foreman in a lumberyard as he should, and knew he was at risk of losing his position. Alma moped without speaking to him, missing Serena terribly. An expert at ignoring his conscience, Donald barely spared Serena a thought.

I'm glad she's gone. I'm out from under Bishop's debt, I no longer have to pay for her food, her useless books. Yup, life is grand. So he told himself as he drank himself into a stupor, not seeing the notice from his employer on the table near his elbow.

Sensing Alma's eyes on him, Donald roused himself enough to blink at her. She stood in the doorway, her arms folded, her eyes once more judgmental.

"Go 'way," he ordered, his words slurred.

Alma ignored him as much as he ignored what he didn't want to face, and stepped closer, looming over him.

"You lost your job," she snapped, fear etching her voice. "You drink, you can't work. We are going to lose our *home.*"

"Nonsense." Donald buried his nose in his glass.

Picking up the notice, Alma wagged it in front of his bleary eyes. "You got fired," she cried. "What are you going to do?'

Donald hiccupped, gazing owlishly at her.

"You drunken sop," she hollered. "You sold my daughter to that fiend, and now I have nothing. You promised to take care of me, and now look! You can't take care of yourself. I lost my *daughter*, Donald, don't you care about that?"

"Hu – Hubert will care for her."

Her palm smacked hard against his cheek. His spittle struck the lamp and sizzled there, and his whiskey sloshed over the rim of his glass. "Hey," he grumbled, his head spinning, his eyes unable to focus. "You'll spill – spill my drink."

"I heard the truth about that monster you sent her to. I hate you."

Alma might have continued with more of her harangue had the front door not crashed open in that moment. Donald blinked as two big men wearing overcoats, gloves and hats pulled low over their eyes stepped into the room. From a distance, he heard Alma scream.

"Now, look here."

Donald tried to rise, to demand why these men entered his home and accosted his wife, but the hard fist in his gut sent him reeling back onto the sofa. Coughing, gagging, he thought he'd vomit all the lovely whiskey he had imbibed. *What a shame that would be.*

Another hard blow to his jaw snapped his head around. *Why is everyone hitting me?* The next knocked him insensible.

～

Donald woke in a puddle of his own vomit. Groaning, smelling the putrid stench, he pushed himself upright, and rolled away from the noxious mess on the floor in front of his nose. Grimacing in disgust, he gazed around, hardly able to see through his blurry vision.

"Alma?" he called, blinking as he tried to wipe the nasty mixture of his supper the previous night and whiskey from his shirt. Instead, it clung to his hands, sticky, repulsive. He got to his knees, and finally to his feet, staggering, the smell following him while he wandered from room to room, calling for his wife.

"I'm sorry, Alma," he said, leaning against a doorframe. "Please come out. Talk to me."

Alma didn't come.

Dimly he recalled the big men, their gloves, their hateful eyes. "Alma?" he cried, frantic now, running, stumbling, searching for his wife. "Alma?"

He did not find her.

CHAPTER 9

Strolling beside the river with Nartan, Serena gazed across its broad expanse. After two weeks of living with his people, sharing Gouyen's wickiup, she finally started feeling at home among them. Under the peaceful skies, she did not miss New York, and her longing to return home slowly faded. In Nartan, she found a constant companion, a friend, and someone she could confide in.

"Your people don't look at me as though I'm strange any longer," she said.

"They are coming to accept you," Nartan replied. "They see you working as hard as any of the women."

Serena laughed. "I will admit using an animal's brains to cure a hide disgusted me at first. But Grandmother has been patient in teaching me."

Why it seemed so natural to begin calling Gouyen "Grandmother," baffled Serena, but she accepted it just as she enjoyed Nartan's company. She had also made a firm friend in Cocheta, who also spent time teaching her how to sew beads into their clothing, skin an animal, and turn the leather into soft clothing.

Though Cocheta spoke no English, and Serena's Apache was in its infancy, the two giggled as they worked, talking in their native languages and laughing over their inability to understand one another.

"Did you like the stew I made, Nartan?" she asked, glancing up at his face.

One thing she had learned about these people was that they never lied. Thus, when she caught the embarrassed expression that crossed his face, she knew her cooking was not quite up to standards.

"Don't answer that," she told him hastily when he hesitated.

He took her hand, smiling. "You are not used to our ways, but you learn quickly."

"I am trying," she replied, liking the feel of her hand in his. "I wasn't considered a decent cook even among my people. I will get better, I promise."

"Grandmother speaks highly of your skills," he told her. "Even my father is impressed with how quickly you are learning."

Though she seldom spoke to the chief, Mangas, Serena liked his self-assured manner, his kindness toward her even if he remained distant and aloof. She suspected he was waiting judgment on her. "Should I return to my people, Nartan?"

She felt his jolt at her question and met his dark eyes when he stopped walking. He did not let go of her hand. "Do you want to leave the village, Serena?"

"Not really," she answered truthfully. "But I don't belong here. Your people are very kind, and I appreciate what they have done for me. What *you* have done for me. But is this where I should spend the rest of my life?"

She saw her words troubled him, for his brows furrowed as he gazed across the barren land, pocked with mesquite and prickly pear. "It is possible for you to become one of the people," he finally said. "If that were to happen, you may choose a man for your husband."

"And would that man want to marry me, a white woman?"

"Yes. You have drawn the eye of many a warrior."

"I thought they stared at me because I am not an Apache."

He laughed. "They speak of your beauty, your hair of fire. They see you are growing skilled in such a short time among us."

"If I chose to stay here," Serena asked, "how do I become an Apache?"

"You may be adopted by a family. You will have parents, siblings."

That statement, of course, made her think of her mother. Being among the villagers, Serena had not written to her as she had promised. Guilt stabbed at her, for she knew how worried Alma must be.

"I have only a mother in New York," she admitted. "No brothers or sisters. It would be lovely to have a real family."

"Do you miss her?"

"Very much."

"But not enough to return to New York?"

That was the question troubling her the most. Yes, she did miss her mother. But she had come to Texas to marry, to raise her own family, and her mother understood that. Now that she had spent time living a cleaner, more simple life, despite the strangeness, Serena did not want to go back to the busy, filthy, noisy New York.

"No," she said softly, "I don't want to return there. It was my home once. It's not any longer."

~

Sweating under the intense heat, Serena wiped her brow with the back of her hand and continued to scrape away the flesh that remained on the deer hide. Thinking back to her old life, she chuckled to think that she had never once thought she'd enjoy such work. Yet, she did enjoy the skills she learned and liked contributing to the welfare of the village.

Cocheta tapped her arm and pointed. Glancing in the direction she indicated, Serena observed the dark thunderheads on the western horizon. "A storm," she said in her halting Apache.

Nodding, Cocheta repeated the word "storm" in English. Resuming her work, Serena wondered if that was the reason for the absurdly hot day. While she had grown used to the dry heat of Texas, on this day, the temperatures had soared.

"It is not yet the rainy season," Gouyen commented as she sewed beads onto a shirt. "That storm will be fierce."

"I hope it cools the air," Serena replied. "The rain will feel good."

Gouyen repeated what she said to Cocheta in Apache, so the girl could follow the conversation. Serena listened closely, trying to memorize the words. She wanted to learn to speak the language as so many of the people did not speak English.

The sound of hoofbeats approaching had her looking up from her work.

Nartan and his friend, Bodaway, rode up to rein their horses in, gazing at the women with identical grins. Serena liked Bodaway. He always seemed to have a smile for her, and never failed to be cheerful no matter the circumstance. Cocheta was deeply in love with him and paused in her work to gaze at him with such adoration that Serena gave her a friendly shove.

Cocheta grinned and said something in Apache. Serena glanced quizzically at Nartan for a translation. "She said 'you need to fall in love,'" he told her.

I think I am well on my way. Serena felt her face heat as she looked away from Nartan's handsome face, and his dark eyes that always seemed to know what she was thinking. *Does he know that I am attracted to him? That I dream of him at night?*

Nor did her growing feelings for him stem from Nartan saving her life. Many men of the village caught her eye, yet none drew her to them the way Nartan drew her. *I think he is attracted to me, too.* She constantly watched for him when he was gone, and craved his nearness, the touch of his hand.

"It is our turn to guard the herd," Nartan said, his gesture indicating Bodaway.

"Return with a hearty appetite," Serena said, glancing up with a sly smile. "Grandmother will be teaching me to cook."

Bodaway made a face, then laughed while Nartan grinned down at her. "Perhaps Grandmother will do most of the work."

Serena stuck her tongue out at him as the two warriors reined their horses around and galloped away. "Your cooking is not so terrible," Gouyen told her, still placidly sewing. "You only scorched the meat once."

"It was also my first time cooking over a campfire," Serena reminded her. "I have learned much since then."

Thunder growled in the distance, and a freshening breeze brought not just a breath of cooler air, but also the scent of rain. Serena glanced up at the cloud bank, not so distant any longer. "That storm is moving fast."

"Yes," Gouyen agreed. "It will bring much needed rain. I would have you go to the river, Serena, and bring water into my wickiup."

"Of course, Grandmother."

Rising from her knees, Serena picked up the leather pails from beside the wickiup and headed through the village to the river. A few people smiled at her and greeted her in Apache, and she returned it in their language. Thunder grumbled again, louder this time.

Bending at the water's edge, Serena glanced at the children playing on the river's bank. A few waded into the shallows, screaming with laughter, splashing one another. Filling the pails with the water, she set them down as thunder cracked sharply. The ground beneath her moccasins trembled, and she glanced around in confusion.

The children seemed to notice nothing, continuing their play. Beginning to wonder if it was her imagination, Serena started back with the water, then heard the distant rumbling. Alarmed, not knowing what caused it, she stopped, and stared.

Upstream, the river rounded a bend, and she observed nothing unusual. However, among the wickiups, people paused in what they were doing just as she had, then several ran toward her, yelling words she couldn't catch. At first, she thought they were calling to her, and she took a few paces toward them.

Then she realized they were not hollering at her, but at the playing children. Fear and distress filled their expressions, and Serena turned back to the children. A few of them obeyed, climbing up the embankment, but one young boy of about four or five years of age continued to play. He stood waist deep in water, reaching down to pluck stones from the river bottom.

At the same instant, a wall of water cascaded around the bend.

People yelled, beckoning wildly. Others ran toward the river, and the youngsters climbing up the bank. The toddler in the river paid no heed to his danger.

"Get out," Serena screamed at him, running toward him.

The boy glanced up at the sound of her voice. As she had yelled in English, he had no idea what she said. The Apaches were still too far away, and she heard a woman scream. The closest adult to the boy was dashing through the shallows toward him, but Serena knew she would be too late.

The flood struck the little boy and swept him away.

Not bothering to think, Serena dove into the raging waters after him.

Cold water closed over her head, and she couldn't see a thing. Kicking hard with her legs, she broached the surface, taking in a gasp of precious air. The river had her in its grip, tossing her, throwing waves over her head, then dragged her back under.

I'm going to die.

Kicking strongly again, Serena once again surfaced, then saw the boy. He bobbed along with the river's flow, his little arms waving before the river sucked him down. *He's alive!* Serena dove after him, not fighting the water, but letting it carry her downstream. Swimming, she kicked with her legs and stroked with her arms, hoping that she traveled faster than the child.

Luck seemed to be on her side when his small body got hung up on a boulder for a moment, and he tried to hang onto its smooth sides. She gained on him before the rushing water hurtled him around it. But when she was close enough to nearly grab him, the river sucked him under.

Holding her breath, Serena dove, swimming as hard as she could. Under the water, even with her eyes open, she saw nothing. Reaching, her fingers touched cloth, and she gripped tightly. Still under the water, she yanked the boy toward her, holding onto him with her arm around his waist.

Rising, she surfaced again, taking the child with her. Gulping air, Serena fought to swim to the bank. In her arm, the boy lay limp, not moving, and she couldn't tell if he breathed. *Please, God, don't let me have just saved a corpse. Let him live.*

As though God answered her, the river suddenly calmed. Serena swam to the shore, still praying, as she dragged herself and the boy onto the bank. Only then did she hear the sound of galloping hooves, the cries and shouts of people. She caught a fast glimpse of Nartan on his black and white pony as she pressed her ear to the boy's face.

He wasn't breathing.

Turning him over her arm, she pushed on his back, trying to expel the water from his lungs. "Breathe," she cried, using the heel of her hand to pound between his little shoulder blades. "Breath, please. Breathe."

Aware of people surrounding her, Serena ignored them, continuing her efforts to get the boy to breathe. Water ran down from her hair into her eyes, but she continued to push on his back. At long last, he coughed, gasped, and vomited up water.

"Thank you, God," Serena cried, turning him over to hug him as the child began to wail. "Thank you, thank you."

Nartan squatted beside her just as a woman pushed through the crowd and grabbed the wailing boy from her arms. Serena gazed up, recognizing her, though she couldn't remember her name. Obviously, she was the toddler's mother, for she wailed and cried alongside him, holding him tightly.

"You saved him."

Serena glanced at Nartan, who drew her into his strong arms and held her nearly as tightly as the woman clutched her baby. Closing her eyes, Serena breathed deeply, tears burning her eyes.

"I thought I was going to die," she whispered. "I thought we both were."

"You did not," Nartan murmured, his hand stroking her back. "But he would have died had you not jumped in to save him."

"No one else was close enough."

Opening her eyes, Serena gazed up at Mangas, who stared down at her solemnly. "No one else could have gotten to him before he drowned," he continued. "You have brought yourself much honor with your bravery."

"I didn't feel so brave," she replied, turning to watch the mother rejoice in her child's safety, several others surrounding her. "I just knew I had to get that boy out."

Nartan stood up and brought Serena up with him, his arms still around her. Several of the villagers spoke to her, smiling, touching her, as Nartan led her through them toward his pony. Though it was hardly cold, Serena shivered under the cool wind from the approaching storm.

She supposed she trembled from the reaction, her close brush with death. The clouds had reached the sun and obscured it as Nartan picked her up and set her on his horse. Not far away, she saw the rain slashing down as the squall grew closer.

"What happened?" she asked as Nartan led the horse toward the village.

"A flash flood," he explained. He pointed toward the rain. "Higher up, the river, the storm dumped much rain into it, thus it washed down onto us."

Serena glanced back to see the Apaches following, hurrying to get back to the village before the storm struck. The boy and his mother had both stopped crying, but she still carried him. Finding Serena watching her, the mother called something, waving.

"What did she say?"

Nartan glanced back, over his shoulder. "She thanked you, and said she owes you a life."

Serena turned back. "No. She owes me nothing."

CHAPTER 10

Outside the wickiup Serena shared with his grandmother, Nartan waited to give Serena time to change into dry clothes before he and Mangas entered. The storm was upon them, the heavy wind slanting the cold rain sideways. At Gouyen's call, he ducked inside with Mangas at his heels.

Wrapped snugly in a blanket, Serena offered him a weary smile as she unbraided her still dripping hair. He noticed that she still shook, and he hoped she had not gotten sick. He folded his legs and sat down, his father beside him.

"You are shaking," Nartan said, watching Serena carefully.

"It is the effects of nearly dying, Grandson," Gouyen told him, filling a metal cup of hot water from the pot over the small fire, then added herbs. She gave it to Serena with the order to drink it.

The storm howled outside, the rain lashed the wickiup and made it creak under the onslaught. But as it had been sturdily built, it withstood the storm's fierceness and no water dripped from above. Mangas also watched Serena with a small frown as though he, too, worried about her.

"There is already talk of adopting you, Serena," he said.

Her green eyes widened over the rim of the cup, and she swallowed her drink too quickly, coughing. "What?" she managed at last.

"You have brought our village much honor," Mangas continued. "If you wished to be adopted, there are families who would be happy to have you become a member of their family."

Nartan grinned at the astonishment on her face. "I hope you will say yes," he told her.

Serena lowered the cup. "I think I would like that."

"You would be given a new name at the ceremony," Mangas said with a grave nod. "In this ceremony, you will be symbolically born an Apache, and given an Apache name."

"She of the Fiery Hair," Nartan suggested with a laugh. "It is perfect for you."

"Say it in Apache."

Nartan did so and listened as Serena repeated it back. "Can I still keep 'Serena' as my name as well?"

83

"If you wish.'

"So who would like to adopt me?" she asked, her eyes on Mangas.

"Kuruk and his wife were the first to speak of it," Mangas replied. "Their children are grown and have children. It is their grandson you saved."

"Oh." Serena finished the brew in her cup. "That would make his mother my sister."

"Yes. I think she would be pleased, but I do not know as the storm drove everyone to shelter."

"I like Kuruk," Serena said with a smile, her eyes shining in the light of the small fire. "He was kind to me right from the start."

Mangas nodded, smiling a little. "He fully approved of you, especially after hearing of your courage in fighting Bishop. There is bad blood between Kuruk and Bishop."

"Then he and I have much in common."

Nartan noticed she had stopped trembling and ran her fingers through her long hair to help it dry. "You want Kuruk and his wife to become your parents?"

"Yes," she answered. "I'm glad I helped his grandson."

Mangas cocked his head, apparently listening to the storm outside. "I will inform Kuruk of this. We can hold the ceremony tomorrow. There will be much feasting and dancing, for a life was saved today."

As they waited for the storm to pass, the four of them spoke of what was expected from Serena at the ceremony. She asked a few questions while Gouyen added wood to the small fire and started cutting vegetables into the pot of hot water. Though Serena tried to help, Gouyen waved her back. "You will cook later."

The storm gradually passed by, but they remained inside to eat the hot delicious food Gouyen prepared. Nartan sensed dusk approaching and wondered if Serena would walk with him. He wanted to spend some time alone with her, and perhaps find out if she liked him as much as he liked her.

Serena agreed, and as people sat around cook fires eating their evening meals, feeding their children, Nartan took her hand and strolled with her near the quiescent river. The rain left behind a strong scent of sage and mud, and their moccasins squished as they walked. Coyotes yipped in the distance, and an owl flew low over their heads.

"I am very glad you decided to become one of us," he began, nervous in the pit of his stomach.

"I suppose I came west looking for a new home, a new opportunity," she replied. "I had no idea it would be among the Apache."

Find your courage, warrior. Nartan drew a deep breath. "I am hoping, once you are ready for a husband, you would consider me."

Serena stopped, gazing up at him. "Do you mean that?" she asked, her voice low.

"I do."

At her continued silence, Nartan grew worried that she found him objectionable, that she discovered another man more worthy of her hand in marriage.

"You are everything I have searched for in a wife," he said, his stomach in knots. "As an Apache, you can select a man, and if he is interested, then you can marry him. If there is another you prefer, I will step aside—"

Under the dim light, he saw her teeth gleam as she smiled. *Does she mock me? Does she not understand our ways?*

"Will you stop talking and kiss me?"

Stunned for a moment, Nartan stared at her, then her hands slid up his chest to his neck. Serena pulled his head down, then he found himself kissing her. Wild thoughts and emotions ran through him as he pressed his lips against hers, the topmost was the knowledge that she cared for him as much as he cared for her.

She told me in a kiss. Too soon for his happiness, Serena broke away from him, but rested her face against his chest. His arms around her small shoulders held her close, and he loved the feel of her against him.

"I was hoping you were falling in love with me," she said at length. "I was afraid you didn't care for me beyond friendship."

"I fell in love with you when I first saw you in the mesquite tree."

Serena straightened, laughing. "I confess it took me longer than that. I didn't know it until I came out of Grandmother's wickiup that first day, and saw you standing there."

Taking her hands, Nartan stared down at her. "You will make me the happiest of men."

⁓

Serena's adoption ceremony took place late in the afternoon. The feast and dancing took place shortly after, and all day long, Nartan scarcely saw her. Grandmother, her new mother to be, and her new sister spent the day with her to get her prepared. Nartan and Bodaway went hunting and brought in a pair of large wild pigs to add to the feast.

Women took the beasts from them, and set to work skinning and butchering them, skewering chunks over fires to begin cooking. Nartan tried to catch glimpses of Serena, but she was well hidden in Grandmother's wickiup.

Bodaway laughed at him. "Now you know what it is to be in love. I am very happy for you, brother."

"And she feels the same way." Nartan laughed for the sheer exuberance of being in love. "I am a very fortunate man."

As neither he nor Bodaway would take part in the ceremony, Nartan stood beside his friend as Serena was born again into the Apache and given a new name – She of the Fiery Hair. Serena rolled it off her tongue several times as she embraced her new family, including the nephew whose life she saved.

She sat between Nartan and Kuruk at the feast, trying to speak in her new tongue, and laughing when she failed utterly. After the feast, the women danced around a fire, singing prayers to the creator, the mother earth, and all the spirits.

Kuruk leaned toward Nartan as they watched to women dance. "You and my daughter are to marry?" he asked.

"Yes," Nartan replied with a grin. "I have wealth in furs, bows and arrows, to pay for her."

"Ah, she will not come cheap, my son," Kuruk told him with a grin on his ancient face. "After all, she brought honor to our people. She is brave and will count coup upon her enemies."

In a wild panic, Nartan hoped he had enough to satisfy Kuruk, and wondered if he would have to borrow items to pay his debt. Then he saw the humorous gleam in Kuruk's eyes, but he didn't know if the old man was teasing him or not.

I will go into debt to have Serena. I am a good hunter. I will pay it back with the buffalo hides and meat when the rains come. I can make bows, arrows, I will tame horses. Serena will be my wife, and we will be happy forever.

CHAPTER 11

Emerging from Gouyen's wickiup, as she had not yet moved in with her new parents, Serena stretched and yawned. She had feasted and danced the entire night, giddy with excitement about her new future, her family. *I have sisters, a brother, a father and mother.* Alma's image came into her mind, and she felt no small guilt at enjoying the prospects of her new adopted family when her blood mother still needed her.

Striding to the cookfire, Serena added wood, and built up a flame, then set a pot of water over it to heat. Grandmother liked her hot herbal brews in the morning, although they were not quite what Serena thought of as tea. *They help my aged bones,* Gouyen had told her.

Around the village, the women and children emerged from their homes, busy building their own fires, preparing breakfast. Laughing, calling out her new name, several children waved at her. Serena grinned and waved back. Only when she turned back to her fire did she see the horse and rider approaching.

The horse came at a walk. Serena stared, transfixed, her stomach tightening with dread. She had almost forgotten him in her new happiness, among her adopted people, and thought he had forgotten all about her. Or believed her dead.

"Hello, Serena," Hubert called, lifting his derby from his gray hair. "You look like a fool Apache dressed like that."

Fury at his audacity to come here, to grin at her as though they shared some secret, to interfere with her happiness.

"What do you want?" she snapped.

By now, the white man's arrival at their village roused the Apache. Warriors leaped aboard horses and galloped forward, rifles in their hands. Nartan was one of them, as was Mangas and Kuruk. Dogs barked, and children were ushered back into shelter. Wishing she had a weapon in her hand, Serena strode forward to stand beside Nartan's horse.

"I want you, my dear," Hubert called.

"No," Serena growled. "I'm not going back with you. I will not marry you."

"You should know better than to come here, Bishop," Kuruk

said. "You were warned once. I have the right to kill you, and the white man's laws will step aside."

Hubert went pale as Kuruk paced his horse forward. "I came for the girl," he yelled. "Give her to me, and I'll never trouble you again."

"This woman is now my daughter," Kuruk told him calmly. "You want her, you go through me."

"She will be my wife," Nartan snarled. "You shall not have her."

"So be it."

Hubert glared at them and replaced his hat. "Serena, come with me and I will not kill your mother."

Serena clenched her jaws to keep them from gaping. "My mother is in New York, far from your evil hands."

"No, my dear, she is my hostage. I had her brought from New York by train, and she has been my guest for the last three days."

"You lie," she hissed, her eyes flattened.

"Then how did I obtain this?"

Hubert reached into an inner pocket of his coat and drew out a necklace. A pendant, a locket with a small snip of Serena's hair in it, one that Alma never removed from her neck. Serena's anger fled, and it its place came fear.

"You would not dare hurt her," Serena grated, her fists clenched. "You would hang if you did."

"Only if I got caught, my dear," Hubert replied loftily. "There are so many places to hide in the West—the law can't find them all."

Her mind whirling, Serena pondered and discarded idea after idea, and knew them to be too risky for her mother's safety. "I should have my father shoot you off your horse."

"Then you sentence your mother to death by starvation," he said, his tone cool. "You will never find her without me. Come now. Get on a horse and come with me."

Before she said a word, Nartan slid down from his pinto, and took her hand. "Go, She of the Fiery Hair," he murmured. "He will not have you. But by going with him now, you can save your mother."

"What will you do?"

Nartan smiled and bent to kiss her. "I will be there when you need me."

Deftly, he slid a short double-edged dagger into her hand even before he stopped his kiss. With Nartan's tall frame hiding her from Hubert's view, Serena quickly hid it in her sleeve. Then he picked her up and put her on the pinto. Gazing down at him, Serena saw the love he had for her in his dark eyes. "I love you."

"As I love you," he replied. "I will marry you."

Nudging the horse into a walk, Serena cautiously approached Hubert. "You ride in front," she ordered. "I'll follow."

Hubert said nothing, then reined his horse around to ride toward El Paso. Serena kept the pinto several lengths behind him, then turned to watch the village, and her people, fade from view. Pulling the knife from her sleeve, her eyes on Hubert's back, she lifted her leg and her skirt, and slipped it into her tall boot.

She straightened just as Hubert looked around. "So they adopted you, eh? The Apache never were very smart."

Deciding not to rise to his bait, Serena kept a watchful eye on him, ready to kick the pony into a gallop at the first threatening move he made. But Hubert rode on, urging his horse into a trot, then a canter, Serena following suit.

"I want my mother's necklace back," she called.

She received a barking laugh in return.

Expecting him to lead her to his house, Serena was not far wrong. Hubert led her past his house, riding toward what looked like an old hut a few miles beyond it. It was not a hut, as it turned out. It was the entrance to an old mine. Hubert reined in and halted, staring at her. Serena halted the pinto, watching him warily.

"Your mother is in there," he told her, jerking his head toward the entrance. "Go get her."

"And have you shoot me in the back?"

"I'm not even armed," he replied. "Call to her. See if I'm lying to you."

Not taking her eyes off of Hubert, Serena raised her voice. "Mother?"

Alma's faint reply seemed to echo from the mine. "Serena?"

Fear and relief warred within her. "I'm here, Mother. Everything will be all right."

"I don't know where I am. Help me."

"I will get you out of there, Mother. I promise."

Still sitting on the horse, Serena eyed Hubert. "What now? I just go in and get her?"

"That's the idea," he answered, that hard shine still in his dirty eyes. "If you can get her out, I'll never trouble you again."

That's when she knew what he planned. The instant he spoke, Serena knew the mine was rigged. Once she went inside to get her mother, he would blow it up. She and Alma would be buried in that mine. *Alive.*

Unless the explosion killed them outright.

And if she refused, he would blow it up anyway, and Alma would die. If she went in, he would blow it. There would be no proof he had killed them, and the word of the Apaches might not be listened to. Hubert would escape with the blood of two murders on his hands.

"You monster," she hissed.

Hubert shrugged. "I have no desire to kill your mother. You go in, fetch her out, and then we'll talk."

"Talk? You brought her all the way from New York to *talk?*"

"I had to find some way to get your attention."

Serena smiled. "Then you go in and get her. I'll wait here, and then we'll talk."

"My house," he said. "My rules. Go get her."

I have to kill him. Nartan and the Apache will be following, but I cannot wait for them. He might choose to blow it up, just to see my agony, my grief. Without much pressure on the pinto's ribs, Serena got him to step aside, as though he were restless.

Now the horse stood between Hubert and her moccasin with the knife in it. She permitted defeat and fear to cross her face, and she gazed at the mine's entrance as though willing herself to dismount and go in. Then she let herself slump, her shoulders rounded, as if Hubert had broken her.

"All right," she told him, forcing tears into her voice. "I'll go in. God help me."

As though to slide off the pony's right side rather than the left, Serena reached down and slipped the knife from her moccasin. With the hilt in her hand, the blade flat against her wrist, she straightened, but kept her head bowed.

"What's taking so long?" Hubert complained. "All I want is to talk. Bring her out, and we three will come to an agreement. In exchange for you accepting me as your husband, I will release your mother, unharmed."

He looked at her with contempt. "And you will wear a proper dress, not that ridiculous Indian garment."

"All right."

Lifting her head slightly, Serena judged this was her best chance. Hubert watched her, yet there was no caution, no respect in his eyes. He believed he had her cowed, and in his arrogance, he never expected her to fight. *You should have learned your lesson.*

With a wild Apache cry of challenge, Serena kicked the pony into a gallop, straight at Hubert. In shock, he gaped for a moment before reining his horse aside. As Serena galloped past him, she slashed him across the face with the blade.

Hubert cried out, blood spurting from beneath his hands. He swayed in the saddle as Serena reined the pony around and charged again, the knife now aimed for his back. At the last instant, Hubert wheeled, his arm raised, and struck Serena across her chest.

The blow knocked her from the pony. She landed on her back and shoulders, the wind torn from her lungs. Through the swirling dust, she saw Hubert dismount from his horse and slap the beast on the rump. It bolted on the heels of the pinto, and Serena, trying to drag air into her lungs, watched Hubert advance on her.

"You're so stupid," he grated, pulling back his boot to kick her in the face.

Serena dodged by rolling aside. Staggering to her feet, she held the knife out, ready to stab or slice any bit of Hubert that came within reach. He hesitated, blinking, blood still gushing from his lacerated cheek. Serena curled her upper lip in a snarl.

"Come on," she hissed, unable to suck in much air. "Let's finish this."

Hubert strode forward, his arrogance unwilling to let him believe a mere woman, a tiny one at that, could possibly harm him. He made to slap the knife from her hand, and Serena slashed him across the palm.

"Now who's a fool?" she taunted, backing away a step, then another, encouraging him to charge.

Bellowing, Hubert ran forward. Serena ducked to the side, under his reaching arm, as lithe as a dancer, as quick as a striking snake. Her knife cut him across the ribs before she spun around behind him.

He may have been ready for that, as Hubert also turned, faster than she would have expected. His hard hand gripped her wrist above the knife, then twisted. Uttering a cry of pain, Serena dropped the knife. Without letting her go, Hubert struck her hard across the face, then permitted her to drop to the dirt.

"Stupid woman," he spat, striding toward her. "You'll go in that mine, and that's where you'll die."

Her head spinning, Serena tried to fight as he dragged her by her wrist across the ground. Unable to get any leverage, she fought, yelling, kicking, but none of that deterred Hubert at all. *Nartan! Where are you!*

As though in answer to her silent cry, wild whoops rose from all around them. Hooves galloped across the sandy ground; gunfire rocked the desert. Hubert grunted, yet continued to drag her toward the mine. A horseman charged forward, lifting his bow, his arrow nocked. Serena had one swift image of Nartan's savage face, painted for war, before he loosed his arrow.

She heard the sound of the arrow striking flesh.

Hubert stopped. His hand slid from her wrist. Serena scrambled to her feet, staggering away from him as Hubert collapsed at her feet. Nartan's feathered shaft stuck out from one side of his neck, the bloody point on the other. Gasping for breath, unable to truly believe Nartan, and the Apache, were truly there, Serena gaped.

Nartan said her name, seized her around her waist, held her close. All around, she heard the triumphant voices of the Apache, Mangas's as well as her father, Kuruk's. Bodaway laughed, praising Nartan's shot as well as boasting of his own that struck Hubert in the back.

"Mother!"

Serena pushed away from Nartan and ran into the mine. She heard Nartan right behind her, tripping over rocks and rotted timbers, seeing her mother on the ground. "Mother!"

Alma lifted a bruised and dirty face, her hair disheveled and dirty, yet her smile warmed Serena's heart. "I knew you'd come," she murmured.

"Nartan," Serena said, her tone urgent. "Hubert rigged this place to blow. We have to get her out of here."

He didn't answer. Instead, he picked Alma up in his arms, and ran with her back down the tunnel. Serena followed, fearing the place might still blow up even without Hubert to trigger it. She refused to feel safe until she, Nartan and Alma were safely out, and she staggered into the sunlight.

Finding her knife, Serena cut the ropes binding her mother's hands and feet, then embraced her. "Oh, Mother," she cried, near tears. "I'm so sorry he did that to you."

Alma held her close, patting her on the back. "This is not your fault," she whispered. "This is Donald's and Hubert's doing. None of yours."

Straightening, Serena wiped her tears from her face. "Mother," she said, turning to take Nartan's hand. "This is my fiancé. This is Nartan. Nartan, my mother, Alma."

Nartan grinned. "It is nice to meet Serena's other mother."

Alma blinked. "Other mother?"

Serena laughed. "I have another family, Mother. This is Kuruk, my adopted father. I'm an Apache now, Mother. The people adopted me."

Alma's shocked response faded quickly, and she smiled and held Serena's hand. "I have nothing in New York to go back to, Serena. Donald has lost everything. Will your people, perhaps, let me live among them? With you?"

Serena glanced at Nartan, who nodded. "Mangas?"

Mangas cocked his head. "She will be your responsibility, She of the Fiery Hair. I am sure she will do as well among us as you have."

Serena hugged her mother. "You will adjust quickly," she whispered. "And you will be safe."

"I will build a wickiup for her to live in, and will hunt for her," Nartan said as Serena broke away, his eyes on Alma. "I will honor her as you do."

Kuruk pointed into the distance, and the dust raised by the approaching riders. "The sheriff comes. He will come to the truth of the matter and see Bishop for what he is. He will not hold us to blame, and for now, there will continue to be peace between us and the white men."

Serena gazed at Hubert's corpse. "I will testify as to what he did, as will my mother. He is a murderer and a kidnapper, an evil man."

Nartan slipped his arm over her shoulders and held her tightly to him. "He will never trouble us again, my beautiful wife. My brave vixen, who counted coup upon her enemy."

Serena laughed, snuggling deeper into his arms. "When will we get married, Nartan?"

He laughed. "As soon as your father and I agree upon a price. I fear he will turn me into a poor man, as his daughter is so valued among the people."

Serena lifted her head to stare at her father. Kuruk shrugged and grinned.

"He will not be poor for long, daughter. Nartan is a resourceful hunter, and with you at his side, he will gain wealth beyond measure."

The End

CONTINUE READING...

Thank you for reading *A Bride for a Debt!* **Are you wondering what to read next?** Why not read *The Groom's Obligation?* **Here's a peek for you:**

Beau Dawson pulled his horse to a stop at the top of the hill overlooking the family farm. It had been nearly ten years since he'd seen that piece of land. When he'd left this place behind, the War between the States was underway, and he and his father, Jacob Dawson, had been at war as well. His father was for the secession and joining the confederacy, and Beau was against it. Their feelings were so strong, they grew almost violent until Beau decided after a particularly vicious argument that he had to leave the farm—his father was just too pig-headed to see right from wrong.

But now his father was gone. Word that his father had

passed away a few weeks before had finally reached Beau in Texas where he worked as a bounty hunter. Beau thought about ignoring the fact, just continuing to work and live his wandering lifestyle as if nothing had changed, but he couldn't. He worried about his mother and his younger brother.

Beau missed his mother, especially, and wondered how she was doing. He was compelled to see with his own two eyes that she was doing all right. He'd been working with his Uncle James as a bounty hunter in Texas ever since he'd left home. He knew it was time to return, so he told James goodbye and headed back to Arkansas.

Now his gaze took in the prosperous farm below. The house was built in homage to his father's home in Georgia with a wide porch and four white pillars across the front. Behind the house sat a red barn, corrals, and pastures. The ground was undulating, spotted with hickory, oak, and pine trees. He could see the river winding around the land through the trees, steeper hills occupying the opposite side.

It was a beautiful sight. Although he never thought of himself as a farmer, he still swelled with pride as he studied the farm below. It was well-kept and productive. The animals in the corrals look content and healthy. He and his father may have disagreed on a lot of points, but they felt the same about caring for the land and the livestock.

He suddenly sucked in a deep breath. His mother...there she was.

He thought his heart had grown so hard over the past years that it couldn't feel much anymore, but he had to admit strong emotions swelled at the sight of her. He hadn't seen his mother in so long, and he'd missed her. Oh, he'd managed to send a few letters home over the years, and a few letters from her had somehow found him as well, but seeing her now created a lump in his throat.

VISIT HERE To Read More:

http://ticahousepublishing.com/mail-order-brides.html

THANKS FOR READING!

Friends, Don't Miss Any News

If you **love Mail Order Bride Romance, Visit Here**

https://wesrom.subscribemenow.com/

to find out about all <u>**New Susannah Calloway Romance**</u> <u>**Releases!**</u> **We will let you know as soon as they become available!**

If you enjoyed *A Bride for a Debt,* would you kindly take a couple minutes to leave a positive review on Amazon? It only takes a moment, and positive reviews truly make a difference. Thank you so much! I appreciate it!

Turn the page to discover more Mail Order Bride Romances just for you!

MORE MAIL ORDER BRIDE ROMANCES
FOR YOU!

We love clean, sweet, adventurous Mail Order Bride Romances and have a lovely library of Susannah Calloway titles just for you!

Box Sets — A Wonderful Bargain for You!

https://ticahousepublishing.com/bargains-mob-box-sets.html

Or enjoy Susannah's single titles. You're sure to find many favorites! (Remember all of them can be downloaded FREE with Kindle Unlimited!)

Sweet Mail Order Bride Romances!

https://ticahousepublishing.com/mail-order-brides.html

ABOUT THE AUTHOR

Susannah has always been intrigued with the Western movement - prairie days, mail-order brides, the gold rush, frontier life! As a writer, she's excited to combine her love of story with her love of all that is Western. Presently, Susannah lives in Wyoming with her hubby and their three amazing children.

www.ticahousepublishing.com
contact@ticahousepublishing.com

Made in the USA
Las Vegas, NV
17 January 2022